Southwood Books Limited
4 Southwood Lawn Road
London N6 5SF

First published in Australia by Omnibus Books 1998

This edition published in the UK under licence from
Omnibus Books by
Southwood Books Limited, 2001

Text copyright © Emily Rodda 1998
Illustrations copyright © Craig Smith 1998

Cover design by Lyn Mitchell

ISBN 1 903207 20 7

Printed in Hong Kong

A CIP catalogue record for this book is available
from the British Library

*For Valerie, who could make anything grow, with love – E.R.*

*For Lisa, who's been growing for some time – C.S.*

## Chapter 1

Mr Green came up our road one day in June. His coat was torn. His shoes had holes. His hat was bent. He wore old gloves. He looked as if he'd come a long, long way.

"What can I do for you, friend?" asked Dad.

"I need to grow some things," said Mr Green. "Can I borrow your hill for a while?"

Dad looked at the dry, brown hill. "Nothing grows up there. Even when it rains," he said.

"I'll fix that," said Mr Green. "I've got green fingers." He grinned a secret sort of grin.

"Have you now?" said Dad. "Well, you can try."

"I'll give you a present when I go," said Mr Green.

"Make it a new tractor," joked Dad.

Mr Green went up the hill. From
his bag he took a tent, and then a
little spade. The sun blazed down on
the dry, brown land.

"He's crazy," said Mum.

Dad looked up. One small cloud drifted in the sky. "Maybe he'll bring us luck," he said.

## Chapter 2

Mum put food in a basket. "Crazy or not, he has to eat," she said. When I saw her add the last apple from the bowl, I knew she was sorry for Mr Green. Mum loves apples.

I took the loaded basket up the hill. On the other side, Mr Green was patting down two mounds of dirt. When he saw me, he pulled on his gloves.

"Have you been planting seeds?"
I asked.

"Sort of," he said.

I told him seeds needed water.

"Rain is coming soon," he said.

He was crazy. It hadn't rained for
weeks.

I gave him the basket. He was
pleased. He chomped on an apple
while he dug another hole.

"Can I help?" I asked. I felt sorry
for him. His shoes had lost their
laces, and he had only one sock,
full of holes.

"I work best alone," he said.

As I left him, I looked back. He'd taken off his gloves again. He put the apple core in the hole he'd dug. He was crazy. Poor Mr Green.

## Chapter 3

That night it rained. We were very happy.

"He did bring us luck," said Dad, at breakfast.

I didn't think it was just luck.

I crept outside and up the hill. Mr Green sat by his tent, eating bread and cheese. His gloves lay beside him.

His fingers were bright green!

I gasped, and ran back to the house.

"Mr Green has green fingers!"
I told Mum.

"Has he now?" she smiled. "Now,
hurry up for school."

Dad was in the tractor, trying to make it start.

"Mr Green has green fingers!"
I said.

"Has he now?" said Dad. "Have
you been playing on this tractor,
Sam? The starter button's gone."

I rode off to school on my little, rusty bike. The bell had fallen off in the night. But I didn't care. I was thinking about Mr Green.

## Chapter 4

When I got home I went up the hill. Mr Green was by his tent, humming to himself.

I looked down at his garden. A green cloth stretched across it, full of lumps, and pegged down at the sides.

"Is that to keep off birds?"
I asked.

"Birds with sticky beaks," he said.
He tapped his toes together. His
fine shoes shone. His socks were
brown and thick.

"You've got new shoes and socks!"
I said. "But where's your hat?"

"It's around here somewhere," he
said, and he grinned a secret sort
of grin.

Then he gave me back the basket, full of big, red apples.

"They're for your mum," he said. "Picked fresh today."

I ran back down the hill and gave
Mum the apples.

"He grew them, from an apple core," I said.

She smiled and shook her head.

"Apple trees don't grow that fast," she said.

"His do," I told her. "He has green fingers."

## Chapter 5

That night it rained again. I woke at sunrise, went outside and ran up the hill.

Mr Green's things were in a mess. His bag had lost its strap. His belt had lost its buckle. One sleeve was gone from his old coat.

Where was Mr Green? I looked over the hill, and blinked.

The green cloth had been pulled
away. Mr Green was in his garden.
Very strange things were growing
there.

Mr Green was planting his belt
buckle. And the sleeve of his coat.
And the strap of his bag.

I pinched myself, to see if I was
dreaming.

Mr Green brushed off his hands.
Then he picked a nice hat from the
hat bush, and put it on.

I squeaked in shock, and he turned around.

"How can you grow a *hat*?" I yelled.

He wiggled his green fingers.
I ran back down the hill.

"Mr Green can grow *anything*,"
I told Mum.

"Can he now?" she said.

"Just *anything*," I told Dad.

"Because of his green fingers,
I suppose," Dad joked.

"Yes!" I shouted. But they didn't
listen.

## Chapter 6

For two weeks after that, the rain came every night and the sun shone every day. Our grass grew long and water filled our pond. We were very happy.

In Mr Green's garden, strange things grew. Soon all his clothes were new. He had a fine new belt, a strong new bag and a brand-new tent. He even had new gloves.

"Nearly time to go," he said to me one day.

"Have you grown everything you want to grow?" I asked.

"Just about," he said, and he grinned a secret sort of grin.

Next morning, Mr Green was gone.

I went up the hill and looked down the other side at what was left of his garden. I looked for a long time. Then I yelled for Mum and Dad.

Mum stared at the present Mr Green had grown for her, from one apple core.

Dad stared at the present Mr Green had grown for him, from a tractor starter button.

And I jumped onto the present
Mr Green had grown for me, from
an old bike bell.

We were very, *very* happy.

We never saw Mr Green again. But I know he's around somewhere. One day you might see him, but you probably won't know it. He looks just like anyone else.

Except that under his gloves he has green fingers.

**Emily Rodda**

I love flowers, and when our new house was built I wanted a big garden. It would have cost a lot to buy all the plants we needed, so I made new plants grow from old ones. I cut pieces from a daisy bush and planted them in my garden. With a little water, they soon grew. Like magic, I had lots of free daisy bushes!

I've always thought it would be great to be able to grow other things – like TV sets, and chocolate cakes! If I was a *really* clever gardener, maybe I could.

## Craig Smith

Like Mr Green, I have grown a wonderful garden on poor soil, but, unlike Mr Green, it took me many years to do it. I owe my success not to magic, but to lots of compost.

Compost is made from lovely rotting leaves and vegetable scraps and so on, and it's very good for making poor soil better. The only problem is that my compost stinks, so no one likes to be in my garden but me. Even the very nice people next door stay inside when I am gardening!

So, I think I have green fingers – and a rubber nose!

# More Solos!

## Dog Star
Janeen Brian and Ann James

## The Best Pet
Penny Matthews and Beth Norling

## Fuzz the Famous Fly
Emily Rodda and Tom Jellett

## Cat Chocolate
Kate Darling and Mitch Vane

## Green Fingers
Emily Rodda and Craig Smith

## Gabby's Fair
Robin Klein and Michael Johnson

## Watch Out William
Nette Hilton and Beth Norling

## The Great Jimbo James
Phil Cummings and David Cox